D0672927

POCKETY

Pushkin Children's Books
71–75 Shelton Street, London WC2H 9JQ

Original title: *Pochée*
Text by Florence Seyvos and illustrations by Claude Ponti
© 1994, *l'école des loisirs*, Paris

English translation © 2014 by Mika Provata

This translation first published by Pushkin Press in 2014

ISBN 978 1 782690 25 2

All rights reserved. No part of this publication may be
reproduced, stored in a retrieval system or transmitted
in any form or by any means, electronic, mechanical,
photocopying, recording or otherwise, without prior
permission in writing from Pushkin Press

Text designed and set in 13.5 / 23 Chaparral
by Tetragon, London

Printed in China by WKT Co

www.pushkinpress.com

POCKETY

The Tortoise Who Lived As She Pleased

Florence Seyvos
Claude Ponti

Translated from the French by
Mika Provata-Carlone

PUSHKIN CHILDREN'S BOOKS

There was, once upon a time, a tortoise called Pockety. She left the home of her parents when she was still very young, so she could live like a grown-up.

Along the way, she met another tortoise, called Thumb. Thumb had also left his parents' house when he was very young, so he could live like a grown-up.

They instantly became friends. They decided to build a hut together, and that proved a very easy thing to do, because they shared the same ideas, and they agreed on everything.

This hut was one big kitchen which they filled with good things to eat. In the middle, there was a pool shaped like an oak leaf, and just in front of the pool there was a fireplace. At night, they slept on cushions set right up against the fireplace. Sometimes, however, they also decided to sleep during the day and live life during the night. Or not to sleep at all.

One day, while they were having a stroll along the riverbank, a stone fell on Thumb's head, and knocked him out. This made Pockety laugh hard. But Thumb, in fact, had not been simply knocked out—he was dead.

Pockety stayed by Thumb's side for many days, waiting for him to wake up, but he did not wake up.

It began to rain. It rained for several days and several nights, and the river swelled, and its waters

carried Thumb away—and there was nothing that Pockety could do. Thumb's shell grew slowly more distant on the flowing river. Then Pockety went back to the hut.

The pool had overflowed. Pockety scrambled up onto the mantelpiece to sleep. She slept for a very long time, but when she woke up everything was the same. And there was absolutely no sound anywhere. Pockety was so very sad, that she wished she were dead. She began to search everywhere in the damp hut, just in case Thumb had left her a little message hidden somewhere. And then she told herself that if she couldn't find one, and she would certainly not find one, she would be even sadder. So she took a sheet of paper, and she wrote the message herself:

My dear Pockety,

I'm writing you this message just in case a stone should fall on my head one day and you are left alone.

I wanted to tell you that you are not really alone, and that I think of you a lot.

I have left you little presents everywhere for all the rest of your life. Today, there is a delicious wild strawberry that has just ripened right at the bottom of the garden. It is for you.

I really think you are a rather nice girl.

Signed: Thumb

Pockety folded the sheet in four and hid it in a corner. Then she found it. She read it, and she scurried outside to the bottom of the garden. She picked the wild strawberry and ate it—it was delicious. Then Pockety decided that the day was over, and went to bed.

The following day was a very beautiful day, but Pockety was still very sad. She wrote a second message from Thumb.

My dear Pockety,

I hope that the wild strawberry was good. Do you know that your shell is a very lovely colour? And, please, would you take care of my mushroom collection?

Thumb

As quickly as she could, Pockety folded the message, hid it, found it again, unfolded it and read it. His compliment regarding the colour of her shell pleased her a lot. But she couldn't help saying afterwards: "You do go too far sometimes, Thumb. It is *your* mushroom collection after all. I can't very well spend *my* life taking care of *your* mushroom collection."

She realized in the end that she had forgotten to give herself a present.

She decided that the day was over, and she went to bed. She dreamt of mushrooms.

The day after, she woke up very early and in a foul mood. She bit at her pillow, and then she went

11

to close all the shutters, because the sun made her eyes sting. She told herself that she needed another message from Thumb, so she began to write:

My dear Pockety,

There is a great big gift for you today; it is a stalk of rhubarb, just as you like them. It is down the far end of the garden.

Pockety realized that she had no idea what to write next. She remained perfectly still for a long moment, her pencil suspended in mid-air. Then she crossed out the beginning of the message, and wrote just below:

12

My dear Thumb,

I know it's not you who writes these messages. And that it isn't you either who sends me gifts. It isn't worth taking the trouble any more. It gives me no pleasure, since I already know it all by heart. Besides, there is no rhubarb at the far end of the garden.

Signed: Pockety

Pockety put her pencil down again. She no longer knew what to do. She walked in circles inside the hut, opened the shutters at the end, and went outside dragging her feet. When she got to the far end of the garden, she suddenly saw a great rhubarb plant. She had never seen it before—it looked as though it must have grown overnight!... The stalks and the leaves were covered with dewdrops, and the sun caused a little rainbow to shine in each one. Pockety was rapt with wonder. Her heart was as heavy as lead, and yet she felt very happy at the same time. She rushed back to the hut, took up her pencil, and wrote:

My dear little Pockety,
    Even if I am not the one who writes the messages, it does not mean that I am not thinking of you.
                                    Signed: Thumb
P.S. As for the mushroom collection, do as you like, it doesn't really matter.

Pockety did not fold this message, nor did she hide it. She re-read it very slowly, and smiled. After that, she decided that the day was over, and she went to bed. She dreamt of Thumb.

The following day Pockety was woken up by loud knocks on her front door. There were voices saying:

"Pockety! Pockety! Open up!"

She got up and went to open the door. It was her parents. She had not seen them for a very long time. She thought that they had grown a little plump.

"How you have grown!" they both exclaimed, entering into the hut with some difficulty. "Oh, how happy we are to see you! Tell us, Pockety, is everything all right with you?"

When she heard those words, Pockety almost burst into tears. She wanted to throw herself into their arms, and say: "No, nothing is all right at all." But at the very last moment, she thought: "My mum isn't Thumb. And my dad isn't Thumb either. They could never take away the pain. There is no point in telling them everything." So she looked up and answered:

"I'm very well. I feel great."

"But you look a little out of sorts," said her dad.

"And it seems to me that it has been a long time since you did any house cleaning," added her mum, looking around her.

"That's because I'm working a lot," said Pockety. "As a matter of fact, I have very little time. But I'll show you around my hut all the same."

Her parents expressed great admiration for Pockety's house, but they were afraid they might be taking up too much of her time. So Pockety politely offered them a small bit of carrot peeling for the way back.

"Goodbye, my little girl, work well," said her dad.

"Yes, Dad," replied Pockety.

"And don't forget to comb your hair," said her mum.

"I don't have any hair, Mum," replied Pockety.

They waved goodbye for a long time. Afterwards, Pockety closed the door of her hut again, and felt that she was really all alone in the world.

She remained standing by the door for a long while, then she decided in the end that the day was over and she went to bed. She slept like a rock and dreamt of nothing.

When she woke up the following morning, Pockety felt the urge to tidy up her hut, because the flood had left a great mess behind. But it took her some time before she could make up her mind. Her right half was telling her: there is no point in tidying up; and her left half was saying: do it. Finally, a little tiny part of herself was telling her to do a third thing, and this was what Pockety wanted to hear. So she listened to it. She was going to collect everything that had belonged to Thumb.

She got up and she began to walk about in the midst of all the mess, looking everywhere. She had, all the same, taken her broom with her, because it would be nice to do some cleaning while she was about it.

She saw Thumb's baseball cap, which was still a little damp, and she put it on her head.

Three steps farther on, she discovered half a gherkin that Thumb had nibbled before going away. She picked it up gingerly, and looked at it as though Thumb might be hiding inside, then she saw Thumb's parasol, which was the leaf of a chestnut tree, and she instantly let go of her broom, so she could take that instead.

With the baseball cap on her head, the parasol in one hand, and half a gherkin in the other, Pockety dared not move any more. So what do I do now? she asked herself.

She was tempted to declare the day over
and go to bed. But it was impossible. Not with a
parasol and half a gherkin in her hands; it was far
too uncomfortable. And how could she possibly
close an eyelid with a soggy baseball cap on her
head? Pockety then suddenly remembered that
the point of making a collection was to arrange it
somewhere.

She let out a sigh of relief and began to search for the right place for it.

She could not find one. The best solution, she told herself, was to put it outside. She went out and placed the parasol and the baseball cap right by the entrance to the garden. Then she considered the gherkin-half carefully. It will rot and disappear, thought Pockety, and, all of a sudden, she swallowed it. All in one go.

Then she went back and began to clean the house, and she did not stop until two days later, when she was done. She was so very tired by then, that she fell immediately asleep.

A funny little noise woke her from her sleep: again, there was someone knocking at her door.

"Whoever you are, for pity's sake, please, open up!" a small voice was saying.

Intrigued, Pockety went to open the door. On the threshold was a small snail, looking a little dried-out.

"I am extremely busy, and I don't want to see anyone," said Pockety to him. "Go away, and don't come back, or, if you really must, come next year."

"I need some cool shade and some water," said the snail. "The sun has blazed so hard these past few days! If you don't let me in, I'll die."

"And so what?" said Pockety.

"Oh, how *can* you be so cruel!" said the snail.

"And you think that by speaking to me in this tone, you will be allowed to come into my house?" retorted Pockety, opening her door just enough for him to slither inside through the gap.

"You have a pool!" the snail exclaimed, wild with joy.

"Yes, and I can put you out the door whenever I feel like it," warned Pockety. "What is your name?"

"Thingummy," said the snail.

"That's ridiculous," said Pockety.

Thingummy, however, paid no attention. He was blissfully moistening his little horns by the poolside.

Afterwards, he let himself slide onto a cushion.

"No!" screamed Pockety, snatching the cushion away.

It was Thumb's cushion. Pockety rushed outside to add it to her collection, then she told herself all of a sudden: I should never have taken his things outside. So she brought the entire collection inside: the parasol, the cushion, the baseball cap. Thingummy was staring at her, pop-eyed.

"So what do we do now?" he asked.

"We sleep!" said Pockety. "The day is over."

"But it's barely just begun!" protested Thingummy.

"It's that or drying out in the sun, you choose," said Pockety.

"Well, all right, then," said Thingummy. "By the way, what is *your* name?"

"Pockety, but I would rather you did not call me anything at all."

"It suits you," said Thingummy.

"Go to sleep," said Pockety.

Thingummy fell asleep almost instantly. Pockety, however, could not find sleep at all. She took a pencil, a sheet of paper, and began to write:

My dear Thumb,

Thingummy gets on my nerves.
What should I do?

Signed: Pockety

And right underneath, she wrote:

My dear Pockety,
*   I don't know.*

Signed: Thumb

Pockety let out a sigh. She looked at Thingummy who was smiling in his sleep. A soft shrill snoring escaped from his nostrils. Pockety felt so infuriated, that she had the urge to go and give him a good nudge with her paw.

The first thing that Pockety saw when she woke up again, was that the sun was still shining as brightly as ever. What she saw next, was that Thingummy was no longer asleep in his place. She sprang out of bed.

"Thingummy, what are you up to?"

"I'm hungry," replied a small voice from the vicinity of the shelves where the food supplies were kept.

"Don't you touch anything," said Pockety. "Come back to bed immediately!"

"I don't feel sleepy at all anymore. I could hardly wait for you to wake up. I was feeling bored. You wouldn't have a little something for me to eat?"

"There's no question of you eating rhubarb, or wild strawberries, or gherkins either," said Pockety. "There's a head of lettuce outside, near the fence."

Thingummy went outside. After a short while, Pockety heard a voice saying: "That's not a very fresh lettuce!"

She sat by the poolside and came to the conclusion that she was the unluckiest tortoise in the whole world. When Thingummy came back, looking well-fed, she asked him:

"When are you going away again?"

"At the first drop of rain," he replied.

Pockety raised her eyes to the sky.

"That's impossible," she said. "You're in the way, I have things to do."

"That's no problem at all," said Thingummy. "Go ahead and do the things you have to do. I won't bother you. Come on. Go ahead."

"No," said Pockety.

"Why?" said Thingummy.

"Because they're secret things."

"In that case, I won't look. Promise," said Thingummy.

And he went to a corner, turning his back to Pockety.

"Come on, then. Do the things you have to do."

Pockety stuck out her tongue at him. A long moment went by. Then Thingummy asked:

"Can I turn around?"

"No," said Pockety.

Another long moment went by. Then Pockety heard a funny little noise.

"What are you doing?" she asked.

"I have secret things of my own to do, you know," replied Thingummy from his little corner.

"You are stupid," said Pockety. "You are stupid, and you are slimy, and you dribble."

"That's just my snail's nature," replied Thingummy. "There are some things, however, that I am very good at."

"Such as, for example?" said Pockety.

"Weeding."

"I don't want you to touch my garden!" said Pockety.

"I never offered to," said Thingummy. And he added: "It would be nice if there were something I could do to keep myself busy, though."

"Very true," said Pockety.

Thingummy thought a little about this. Then he asked:

"You wouldn't happen to have some paper and paints? I'm an excellent painter."

Pockety hesitated.

In the end, she went to fetch what Thingummy had asked for.

"What a beautiful red! What a gorgeous yellow!" he exclaimed, unscrewing the caps of the paint tubes one by one.

"Just paint and be quiet," said Pockety.

She went and sat behind her bed, to better observe Thingummy. He swam in the little puddles of colour in order to mix them, then he wandered lazily across the sheet of paper in every possible direction. He painted for many long hours,

without uttering a single word. Pockety coughed meaningfully several times. Thingummy took no notice of her.

"It's finished!" he exclaimed at last. "It's fabulous, don't you think? I really got it just right."

He jumped into the pool, whose waters now turned red and yellow. Then he came out and he said with a yawn:

"I feel utterly exhausted after that. I think I am going to have a nap. Good night."

The very next instant, he had retracted his horns and was snoring soundly asleep. Pockety realized that the day had come to its end. But on that particular night, she did not want to sleep at all. And she did not want Thingummy to sleep either. Or, perhaps, she wanted to paint an immense picture instead, a very beautiful one, while Thingummy slept, and then really surprise him with it when he woke up.

It was really dark now. Pockety thought of Thumb so that she could make tears spout from her eyes. She made some fall on her pillow, then she made some fall by the feet of Thingummy's bed. But she did not wake him up. Finally, she stood in front of her mirror to watch the tears stream down her face. This comforted her a little, and she fell asleep.

The following day, she was woken up by Thingummy, who was all excited.

"It's raining! It's raining! Look! I'll be able to go out! I'll be able to swim in the puddles and slide down the leaves! And I'll get to see again my parents, my brothers and my friends. I offer you my painting to remember me by. Thank you for saving my life, Pockety. And perhaps we will meet again, who knows!"

By the time Pockety had reached the door, Thingummy was already far away.

Pockety thought to herself that snails could move very fast sometimes. She looked around her to see if he hadn't left anything behind, but there was only his drawing. She took it and tore it up into small pieces.

You couldn't make out anything on that drawing, she told herself, and he had not even drawn a tree, or a sun, or a tortoise for what it's worth. Pockety walked in circles inside her hut. In the end, she took a sheet of paper and wrote:

> *My dear Thumb,*
>> *I am bored.*
>
>>>> *Signed: Pockety*

And right underneath,

> *My dear Pockety,*
>> *Go on a journey.*
>
>>>> *Signed: Thumb*

Pockety put her pencil down again.

37

"I'll go on a journey if I feel like it," she said. "I'm not going to spend my life following the advice of others: work well, comb your hair, go on a journey. I'll do as I like."

She thought hard, in order to work out what she wanted. She realized that she felt a tiny little urge to go on a journey. I am free, she told herself. And she packed her suitcase in a very bad mood. She began by putting inside Thumb's baseball cap, Thumb's cushion and Thumb's parasol. But the parasol was too big for the suitcase, and the suitcase was far too heavy. So Pockety then took Thumb's things out again. It is so complicated packing a suitcase, she told herself. In the end, she put in her suitcase only sheets of paper and her pencil. Outside, the rain stopped and the sky cleared up.

I am off, Pockety told herself, and she closed the door of the hut. The earth smelled good, and the air was mild. Pockety felt her bad mood lifting and flying away. She felt light-footed. She plunged through the trees. Ahead of her she saw a rabbit, and she made a detour, because she didn't feel like striking up a conversation with a rabbit. A little farther on, she noticed a tortoise, and she did not make a detour. The tortoise was lying under a chestnut tree. It looked carefully at Pockety as she drew nearer.

"Good morning, my charming young tortoise," it said.

"Good morning," said Pockety.

"Where are you off to like that?" said the unknown tortoise.

"I am off on a journey," said Pockety.

"And what is your name?"

"Pockety."

"Mine is Nestor," said the stranger. "You know, Pockety, you remind me of a tortoise with whom I built a hut a long time ago. And then, one day, she left, without even saying goodbye."

"She wouldn't have been struck by a stone on the head, by any chance?" asked Pockety.

"That is possible," said Nestor. "She went off with a weasel."

"Phew," said Pockety.

"After that, I built another hut with another tortoise. A very absent-minded tortoise. She set fire to our house while lighting the candles on my birthday cake. This made me terribly angry. But now I regret it. I truly regret it."

And so you should, thought Pockety, who detested people who got angry.

"If you were to come with me to my house, my little Pockety," said Nestor, "I would play the violin for you, and I would recite poems to you to lull you to sleep. Would you like that?"

"I don't know," said Pockety cautiously.

"Your shell is very elegant," said Nestor.

"Thank you," said Pockety.

She could think of no compliment that she

could pay Nestor in return. All she could see, was that he had yellow eyes.

"It's sad to be alone," said Nestor softly. "You need to have someone to look after you."

"Perhaps," said Pockety. "But I have a journey to make. Please excuse me."

And she walked away in zigzags because she felt Nestor following her with his eyes.

While she walked, Nestor's words turned inside Pockety's head. I don't have anyone to look after me, she kept repeating mournfully to herself. It was Thumb who took care of me before. The instant I fell ill, he would make me infusions of verbena. Pockety

thought hard. She knew that it wasn't Thumb's
infusions of verbena that made her well when she was
ill. Before Thumb had been there to take care of her,
she had always got better without drinking infusions
of verbena each time she had fallen sick. In fact, she

did not like verbena infusions all that much. And yet, she suddenly felt a great urge to drink one right then and there. Her throat felt a little prickly. I have to stop thinking about infusions of verbena, Pockety told herself, or I shall come down with the flu.

She crossed a great meadow full of flowers, then she re-entered the canopy of trees. Every time the path she had taken did not please her any more, she changed it. She saw a hedgehog under an ash tree.

When the hedgehog saw Pockety, he began to curl himself into a ball, leaving only the tip of his snout sticking out.

"Good morning," said Pockety very softly.

"Good morning," said the hedgehog even more softly.

"I am on a journey," said Pockety. "I have walked a great deal. Would it bother you if I sat down here for a moment to rest?"

The hedgehog uncurled himself just a little to have a better look at Pockety.

"No," he said.

And he let out a little sigh.

"And would it bother you if I asked you your name?" said Pockety.

"No," said the hedgehog. (He let out another sigh). "My name is Pippin."

"Have you been here long?" asked Pockety.

"Long enough," said Pippin. "My parents asked me to take my seven little brothers and my nine little sisters out for a walk, and to take good care not to lose them. But it is my brothers and sisters who have lost me. First, they blindfolded me, just for fun. Then they buried me in the ground, just for fun. And then they left."

"Oh, how horrid of them!" said Pockety.

"Oh, no, not at all," said Pippin. "There were far too many of us, anyway. I am quite happy

48

where I am. I have built myself a house, and I make blueberry tarts. They are very good. Would you like to taste one?"

Pockety accepted. She went to Pippin's house, and told him her whole story while eating blueberry tart.

"And after I had crossed the meadow, I came into this forest, and after that I saw you, and that's that," she said to finish.

Pippin thought hard for a long moment, then he said:

"That snail called Thingummy, he wasn't really nice, was he?"

"You really think so?" said Pockety.

"I do," said Pippin. "And I also think that your story is a sad one, and that you are a very unlucky tortoise."

49

Pockety helped herself to another slice of blueberry tart.

"Sometimes I actually think I'm rather lucky," she said, "and that I'm quite a nice girl."

"Me too," said Pippin. "I think I'm nice too."

"That doesn't surprise me," said Pockety.

She said goodbye to Pippin, promising to catch up with him soon, and she resumed her journey.

After a while she was thirsty and she stopped by the riverbank. She was stooping down to drink, when she noticed a hole in one of the rocks. And as the hole was exactly her size, she went inside. She discovered then a very beautiful little cave, which belonged to no one. It had two windows and the ground was covered with a carpet of soft mosses.

"If this isn't luck, I don't know what is," said
Pockety. "I have never seen a more beautiful place.
This cave will be my home."

Pockety set down her suitcase.

She told herself that since she had found this cave, it surely meant that there must be other very beautiful empty little homes elsewhere as well, where she could go and live if she wanted to. And this was a very good reason for her to stay right where she was.

She took out her paper and her pencil, and wrote a letter to her parents.

My dear parents,

I have made a long journey, and I have found a beautiful cave by the riverbank, and this is my new home. Perhaps one day I'll go on another journey, but for the time being I am staying here.

Please come and visit me any time you like, it would give me great pleasure to see you.

Pockety

After that, she prepared a batter for pancakes, hung curtains at the windows, and invited Pippin to tea.

"I love pancakes," said Pippin, as he came in. "And I have never had any."

They flipped the pancakes together, each in turn, sending them as high up as possible.

It was a very successful tea party. But towards the end, Pockety felt that she needed to be alone in order to think. It was already nightfall in the forest, and Pippin went back home.

Pockety looked through the window at the tree-branches sketching weird forms in the blackness. Then she pulled the curtains.

She took a sheet of paper, her pencil, and she sat on the ground. She listened to the silence, without moving. She tried to guess what the silence was saying to her. And she began to write.

My dear Thumb,

I am a very cheerful tortoise.

Perhaps now I will no longer cry when I think of you, but I shall miss you always. So, when I feel really sad, I will pretend to cry. Later on, I hope I can forget you just a little bit. But right now, I hope that I shall never forget you.

Signed: Pockety

Epilogue

Tortoises live to a very old age. One day, Pockety celebrated her 111th birthday. Her grandchildren came to visit her and they offered her a parasol. Pockety had seventeen grandchildren, all girls.

Each time they came to see her, the little tortoises made Pockety tell them the story of her life. How she had left her parents' house in order to live like a grown-up, how her friend Thumb had been struck by a stone on the head, and all the rest. Sometimes, this made the youngest of the little tortoises a little sad, and then Pockety comforted them and reassured them. But often, they just roared with laughter.

"A stone on the head! *Pong*!"

On that day, just like every other time, Pockety had had to tell them the story of her life. And the little tortoises had tried to guess the number of pancakes that their grandmother had made in her long life. A thousand, a hundred thousand, perhaps even millions of them.

Towards the end of the tea party, Pockety looked out of the window and saw that one of her granddaughters had gone to sit by the river.

Pockety had a slight preference for this particular tortoise, whose name was Bubble, and who was quite clever.

She went out and sat by her side, to watch the river flow by. Pockety loved doing that.

After a while, Bubble asked:

"You know, grandmother, when I grow up, I'm not going to do things the way you did."

"Is that so?" said Pockety.

"Absolutely," said Bubble. "You see, *I* will have a friend. He will sit next to me at school. He will be very, very good-looking, very, very nice, and very, very clever. He will be just as I would like him to be. And afterwards, we will go on long journeys all the time. And I will always be very happy. And he will never leave me," she added throwing a small blue pebble into the water.

"What a good idea, my little one," said Pockety, looking at the stone sinking down to the bottom of the river.

PUSHKIN CHILDREN'S BOOKS

Just as we all are, children are fascinated by stories. From the earliest age, we love to hear about monsters and heroes, romance and death, disaster and rescue, from every place and time.

In 2013, we created Pushkin Children's Books to share these tales from different languages and cultures with younger readers, and to open the door to the wide, colourful worlds these stories offer.

From picture books and adventure stories to fairy tales and classics, and from fifty-year-old bestsellers to current huge successes abroad, the books on the Pushkin Children's list reflect the very best stories from around the world, for our most discerning readers of all: children.